My Life Journey
by S. B. Alapati

*A collection of **personal** and **spiritual** poems*

Dedication

To my children - may these words lift you when the world feels heavy and remind you that love and hope are never lost.

To every soul who turns these pages - may the poems speak to your spirit, bring solace to your heart, and whisper that you are never truly alone.

Acknowledgement

All glory to God, whose grace carried me through storms, whose light guided my steps when the way seemed hidden, and whose love has been my anchor through every trial.

To those who have walked beside me, offered a hand, a word, or a quiet presence, thank you. May these pages honour the resilience of the human spirit, the power of faith, and the enduring gift of love.

Preface

My Life Journey is more than a collection of poems – it is the heartbeat of my story.

Each piece is a window into the joys, sorrows, struggles, and triumphs that have shaped who I am. From the depths of pain to the light of healing, these poems reflect the real moments of my life: the silence of grief, the echoes of trauma, the hope of faith, and the warmth of love.

I began writing during the time when words were all I had to help me breathe again. Writing gave me peace. It gave me freedom. It helped me remember who I was before the pain, and who I was becoming through it. Many of these poems are rooted in real experiences – my childhood, my years in an abusive marriage, my family, grandkids, friends and working colleagues, the passing of my loved ones, and the quiet beauty of finding peace after chaos.

Each page is a step in the journey. Some may bring tears. Others may offer comfort. But all are honest. All are mine.

Thank you for walking this path with me.

TABLE OF CONTENT

FROM CHILDHOOD TO ADULTHOOD

This section traces the tender beginnings of life – innocence, curiosity, and the steps that led from youthful dreams to the responsibilities of adulthood. It is the story of growth, lessons, and the shaping of identity.

WHEN I WAS YOUNG

A childhood memory,
glowing with light,
my first day of school,
filled with wonder and awe.
At five,
the world was wide and fresh,
not about lessons,
but colour and play.

Those were days of sun and freedom,
when worries hadn't yet learned my name.
I wandered without care,
finding comfort in every corner I knew.

School was a stage of endless stories,
where curiosity bloomed like spring.
Each day held a new surprise,
games, giggles,
the magic of pretend.

Sometimes I hid in invisible places,
waiting for the bell to ring.
The sound meant home,
but first, I'd wait for my siblings,
so we could walk back together.

We'd hop along the path,
singing songs,
we never quite finished,
the sky stretching above us,
like a blanket of promise.

When I was young,
the world shimmered with innocence,
laughter was easy,
and joy needed no reason at all.

THE SWING SET

The old swing set stood,
under the summer sun,
its frame worn but steady,
a throne in my childhood kingdom.

Each day began there,
bare feet on dry grass,
heart light with the promise of flight.

The ropes groaned in rhythm,
a sound I knew by heart,
comforting,
like a voice calling me home.
The wind wrapped around me,
cool against my skin,
whispering that nothing else mattered.

The sea breeze carried,
salt and freedom.
Laughter rang out,
mine, and theirs,
echoing across the yard,
as if joy could live in the air.

We didn't count time then.
We just swung,
back and forth,
higher and higher,
as if we could reach the clouds.
and stay there.

Evening crept in slowly.
The wood creaked softer,
the sky dimmed,
but we held on a little longer,
floating between day and night.

That swing set wasn't just a place,
it was a feeling.
Of being young.
Of being untouchable.
Of knowing the world,
only by how high you could fly.

It lives in me still,
that moment,
that movement,
that magic.

HAPPY TIMES

I used to lie on the grass,
staring up at the sky,
letting my thoughts drift,
wondering what the world looked like,
beyond the clouds.

I remember chasing butterflies,
a small girl with bare feet and tangled hair,
trying so hard to draw a dragonfly,
its wings never quite right.

Sometimes I wonder,
if those moments were real,
but I feel them still,
like echoes of laughter
carried on the wind.

There were nights the moon was so full,
it lit up the whole field,
even the corners usually,
left in shadow.

I remember the sound of mother's voice,
gently calling from the doorway,
before the sun had properly risen.

"Time to get ready," she'd say,
and I would groan,
my body heavy with sleep.

But there was joy in those mornings,
quiet, simple joy.
No burdens.
No fear.
Just the softness of rain on my skin,
and the way I would spin beneath it,
as if the world was made just for play.

AWAY FROM HOME

It was the first time I left home,
Not just the house,
but the people I love.

I stayed with strangers,
who were kind,
but they didn't know me.

At night, I missed everything,
Mum's gentle hands,
Dad's quiet strength,
my siblings' noisy love,
and the steady comfort,
of my grandparents' presence.

The silence felt heavy,
even in a full room,
I felt alone.

No one laughed like we did.
No one remembered,
the small things that make me, *me*.

That's when I understood,
home isn't a place,
it's family.

And no matter where I go,
you stay with me.
In my thoughts.
In my heart.
In every quiet moment,
I wish you were near.

WHERE YESTERDAY STILL LIVES

The scent of dust in the old house,
carries a quiet plea,
a presence, faint but familiar,
like the breath of those who came before me.

Their stories rest,
in faded photographs,
but their voices linger,
in the stillness between heartbeats.

A chipped teacup,
a worn chair in the corner,
these simple things,
hold the weight of lives once fully lived.
Memory stirs, not always clear,
but strong enough to feel.

I see sunlit fields,
through the haze of childhood,
hear the laughter near the stream,
where the water ran freely,
and time moved slow.

Down by the coast,
the waves beat out their rhythm,
on golden sand,
a song of freedom,
a place where I was whole.

Warm skin, salt air,
and that breeze,
that knew my name.
It was home,
in a way nothing else ever could be.

What once held me,
now drifts just out of reach.
And still, it remains.
Not in place — but in me.

Today waits — a blank canvas,
and with all I carry,
I begin again.

JOURNEY THROUGH

In 1973, I packed my bags,
Dreams folded in between the rags.
The family smile, proud and bright,
Their joy a beacon, my guiding light.

The campus buzzed, alive, profound,
New faces, voices all around.
But in the quiet, when day was through,
I'd close my eyes and think of you.

The smell of home, the kitchen's cheer,
The comfort of knowing you were near.
Letters penned in hurried script,
Tears unshed, the pen's ink tipped.

Mother's warm hug, Father's soft advice,
Their pride in me, a sacrifice.
For a while they beamed, I bore the cost,
The feeling of being a little lost.

In 1974, I found my stride,
Yet still, I missed home and the seaside.
Our talks were brief yet filled with care,
Their voices echoed everywhere.

By 1975, the world seemed wide,
I learned to laugh, to grow inside.
But every milestone, big or small,
I longed for home to see it all.

In 1976, the end was near,
The cap and gown, the family's cheer.
Yet in their joy, I still could see,
The part of home they gave to me.

Though years apart, my heart stayed true,
For every step, I carried you.
Through pride and longing, joy, and strife,
Your love has been my compass in life.

DREAM JOB – WINGS OF FATE

I dreamed of skies so vast and blue,
Of soaring clouds and endless view.
To be a flight attendant, free,
To travel far, from sea to sea.

With every take-off, every land,
To touch the earth, both wild and grand.
To see the world, each face, each place,
A life of wonder, joy, and grace.

But fate had woven threads unknown,
A path that wasn't mine to own.
The dream I chased began to fade,
As life revealed a new parade.

A different job, a different role,
A journey still to fill my soul.
Though grounded now, I've come to see,
This path was meant to set me free.

For dreams can change, yet still remain,
A source of growth, a spark of gain.
The world is vast, and I've my share,
In ways I'd never thought to dare.

So here I stand, with heart content,
Embracing what the journey meant.
For thought I've not touched every sky,
My spirit soars: I still fly high.

NEW ARRIVAL

A suitcase full of hope,
and whispers of a promised land,
the stories I heard,
land of *milk and honey*,
but left out the part,
of how much it costs.

I crossed oceans,
for someone not yet born,
chasing a future,
I could only imagine,
a safer place, a softer life,
than the one I left behind.

The streets were busy,
the skyline proud,
but behind the shine was struggle.
No open arms, no waiting hands,
only hours to trade for rent,
and sweat to earn my place.

Family came,
brief shadows in the doorway,
offering smiles before returning,
to their own place.
Love, but no anchors.

Nothing was free,
not bread, not kindness,
not even time.
But still I stayed.
Still, I worked.
For the dream I carried,
a child, unborn, whose feet I hoped,
would stand more firmly,
than mine ever could.

This is not the story I was told.
But it is the one I chose,
And that, too, is a kind of freedom.

YOUNG MOTHER

What did I know at just twenty-one?
A baby in my arms,
and the world unseen.
Fear whispered loudly in every cry,
No guide beside me, no lullaby.

The nurses taught me what they could,
Still, I stumbled more than I understood.
Sleepless nights with no one near,
Just quiet prayers and rising fear.

Anxiety lingered, like breath on glass,
Each moment fragile, slow to pass.
But somewhere deep, a strength awoke,
A silent vow I never spoke.

Through feeds and endless pace,
I found my rhythm, found my place.
The ache of doubt began to fade,
In love's soft cradle, I was remade.

Each routine held me like a song,
And in that bond, I grew strong.
No longer lost, no longer alone,
A young mother, fully grown.

REMEMBERING THE PAST

Bags packed, hearts high,
warm air clinging to our skin,
like the last blessing of home.

The island stayed behind,
but not its song.
It hums in our bones,
a lullaby beneath the noise,
of foreign streets and steel skies.

We traded coconut groves,
for crowded trains,
barefoot days for hours in shoes,
that never quite fit.

Photos curled in old suitcases,
faces we swore we'd never forget,
now blurred, but never erased.

We smiled through letters,
called less often.
Families thinned by distance,
yet roots held firm,
deep in memory's soil.

In winter's chill,
we remember warm rain,
clothes drying on the line,
the way aunties laughed
without apology.

Here, we build with what we carried:
recipes, hymns, names,
that strangers stumble on.
Here, we stay and strive,
because someone must.

And still, the past walks with us,
not to weigh us down,

but to remind us, who we are,
and how far we've come.

THE HOUSE AFTER HOME

Boxes stacked, walls bare once more,
The echoes linger, a closing door.
Familiar streets, now left behind,
Memories woven, soon confined.

A home we made, a life took root,
Neighbours' smiles, the kids' pursuit.
The shops where mornings grew,
The sunset bench with its golden hue.

Yet here we are, on the road again,
Goodbyes whispered like soft rain.
Familiar paths dissolve in haste,
New horizons to embrace.

But oh, the ache of starting afresh,
Learning the streets, the names ahead.
Faces warm, yet still unknown,
Another chance to claim a home.

So, we pack the past with tender care,
For every place, a heart we wear.
Though restless winds may guide our way,
Each home we leave, will always stays.

SCARS OF SILENCE

Here lie the hidden wounds, the untold stories, and the silence that shaped strength. These reflections acknowledge pain while honouring the resilience that rises from it.

WHO AM I?

The question rises in the stillness,
not shouted, just breathed.
Who am I,
when the world goes quiet?

I've worn many faces,
some out of fear, some to survive.
But none ever felt like home.

I watched love from a distance,
felt joy on borrowed skin,
and wondered if God saw me at all.

Pain was patient.
It waited in corners,
sat beside me at night.
And illness,
it stole what I couldn't name,
one moment at a time.

But in the silence,
I heard something else:
a whisper, a presence.

You are Mine, He said, *even here.*
And I wept — not in defeat,
but in release.

Each day still comes heavy.
The chores, the mask,
the echoing rooms.
But somewhere in the mess,
grace lives.
Small. Quiet.
Unmoving.

I dig not for the person I used to be,
but for the one He's shaping now.

A new self, not lost, but becoming.
Not alone. Not forgotten. But held.

ECHOES OF PAIN

A tale unfolds of pain that seeps,
In darkness nights where silence weeps.
Through tear-streaked nights and broken day,
A battered heart in endless maze.

I once was free, a spirit bright,
In love's embrace, in pure delight.
But darkness fell like thunders roar,
And shattered dreams on the cold floor.

Bruised and battered, yet I stand,
With courage in my trembling hands.
I bear the weight of endless strife,
A battered wife, yet full of life.

My spirit, fierce, refuses to break,
In every step, a silent quake.
I longed for peace, a love that's true,
To heal the wound, both old and new.

Through silent prayers, I find the strength,
A beacon guiding me at length.
To rise above the pain and fear,
And wipe away every silent tear.

In my eyes a fire burns,
A fierce resolve it brightly yearns.
To break the chains that bind my soul,
And find again myself made whole.

With every dawn a new chance lies,
To mend my wings, to touch the skies.
No longer trapped, I will learn to soar,
A battered wife, I am no more.

With strength, I find the way to heal,
A love renewed; a life surreal.
In my heart, I will always find,
The power to leave the past behind.

BEHIND THE SMILE

Have you ever carried, a burden unseen?
A silent sorrow, a heart's hidden pain?
I lived with that weight, a constant, cruel scene.
Throughout my marriage, a relentless, aching strain.

I wore a smile, a mask for the world to see,
But underneath, a silent, desperate plea.
Each night, I slipped away to a room dark and still,
To weep in the shadows, my heart's deep wounds to fill.

The emptiness consumed me, in that lonely, darkened space.
My home, a prison, devoid of love and grace.
No one to confide in, no shoulder to lean on,
My pain a secret, a burden to be borne.

I carried that weight, through each passing day,
Hoping for help, that would somehow find its way.
My thoughts raced wildly, in a chaotic, tangled maze,
And in my darkest hours, I longed for death's cold haze.

But then, a lifeline, a glimmer in the night,
God's grace descended, a beacon burning bright.
Hope and comfort flowed, as I knelt down to pray,
And found the strength to rise and face a brighter day.

A HIDDEN STRUGGLE

The world shrinks down, to shades of grey,
A canvas dark, where hopes decay.
The urge to quit, a whispered plea,
To end the pain, and finally be free.

I'm drowning deep, in sorrow's tide,
Alone I stand, with nowhere to hide.
Life's crushing weight, a heavy chain,
Whispering doubts, a haunting strain.

The thought takes hold, a chilling fear,
To end it all, and disappear.
To silence the screams, the inner strife,
And find release, from this hard life.

But pause, dear heart, before I yield,
That voice of despair, must be repealed.
Tend to my soul, with gentle care,
Nurture my spirit, beyond compare.

There's help to find, a hand to hold,
A story yet untold, to unfold.
Believe, dear one, there's hope to see,
In self-compassion, set my spirit free.

MISUNDERSTOOD

Misunderstood, a soul cry out,
In silence, battles, fear and doubt.
A world that fails to see within,
The beauty of a heart's akin.

Words may falter meaning loss,
In tangled webs, emotions tossed.
Yet deep within a truth resides,
A spirit strong that still abides.

Seek not to judge with haste glance,
For underneath there lies a chance.
To bridge the gap that keep us far,
And find the light like morning star.

Misunderstood, but not alone,
A symphony of hearts in tone.
A melody of empathy,
That breaks the chains of apathy.

So, let us strive to comprehend,
The depths of souls, and then extend.
A hand of kindness, love and peace,
To heal the wounds in life's embrace.

For in each tale of misunderstood,
Lies the potential for the good.
To learn, to grow, to empathise,
And see the world through others' eyes.

UNFINISHED BUSINESS

In the corner of the mind, it dwells,
Unfinished business, like tolling bells.
Promises made but left undone,
Echoing regrets one by one.

Words unspoken, deeds unfulfilled,
The weight of them, my heart has chilled.
In the gentle hours, they haunt my soul,
Unfinished business takes its toll.

Yet in the midst of this shadowed plight,
There lies a glimmer of hopeful light.
For in each moment, there's a chance to mend,
To finish what has started and make amends.

So, let us not be bound by past mistakes,
But seize the present, for the sake.
With courage and resolve, let us address.
The unfinished business, and final redress

UNSOLVED PUZZLE

I loved a man,
made of pieces,
some soft,
some sharp,
some lost.

He could be gentle,
eyes calm,
hands careful.
Then,
just like that,
a storm.

Sober,
he was almost whole.
Drunk,
he disappeared.

I tried to hold him,
together.
Tried to fit his pain,
into something I could fix.
But some pieces,
never came home.

Still,
I loved him,
not the version I imagined,
but the man as he was.
Flawed.
Fading.
Real.

Even broken,
he mattered.
And in me,
he still lives.

LIFE STRUGGLE
Tick tock, tick tock,
the clock moves without pause,
time slipping fast,
and memories of the past,
fade slowly in its shadow.

Chasing dreams and comfort,
I found myself,
living a life of quiet struggle.
I stayed silent,
even when the days were hard,
even when the nights felt longer,
than the stars.

It was never what I imagined,
but I learned to bend, to make do,
to build with the pieces I had.
Still, sometimes it was too much.

Friends and family might think,
my path was easy,
but they cannot feel,
the deep ache I carried,
the silent weight of everyday trials.

And yet, in this suffering,
I see the thread we all share,
the quiet endurance,
the resilience of the human heart.

MOTHER'S LOVE, SICKNESS, LAUGHTER AND TEARS

This section captures the heart of motherhood – its joys, sacrifices, struggles, and laughter through tears. It is a testament to the unconditional love that endures even in life's hardest moments.

MY MOTHER – SPECIAL LADY

I haven't seen you for a while,
And my heart aches to see your smile.
Your loving nature, oh how I yearn,
Wishing for the days when love would return.

Mother, you inspired us all,
A guiding light, you stood tall.
Though English words may not be your tune,
Your faith shone bright like the morning moon.

I recall the struggles you faced,
So we could thrive, our dreams embraced.
A mother's love, a boundless stream,
Overflowing with hope, like a cherished dream.

You are the essence of pure affection,
A blessing bestowed, a perfect reflection.
An ocean of kindness, your words so sweet,
Encouragement flows, a rhythmic beat.

I love you, Mother, with all my heart,
Even though I don't say it often enough.
Your spirit lives on, forever near,
In every beat, your love is clear.

MOTHER'S LOVE

In a world of whispers, love profound,
A mother's heart, a treasure found.
With gentle touch, and soothing voice,
She guides her children's loves pure choice.

Through laughter's dance and tearful night,
Her love, a beacon, shining bright.
In every hug, a warmth untold,
A mother's love, more precious than gold.

Through storms and sunshine,
she'll stand strong,
A lullaby, a comforting song.
Unconditional, her love's embrace,
A sanctuary, a sacred space.

In every smile her joy takes flight,
A mother's love, an endless light.
Through ups and downs, in every stride,
Her love, a constant, by their side.

A FIGURE ON THE BED

"This is about my mother."
It is morning...
but the kind of morning that doesn't rise.
The light creeps in,
slow, hesitant,
like it doesn't want to intrude.

She's lying there,
a figure on the bed.
Still. Quiet.
Like she's somewhere between here...
and somewhere I can't reach.

Her eyes — half-open,
not looking *at* me, but *through* me.
Like she sees something,
I'm not meant to understand.

Her hand — the same hand,
that once wiped tears from her face,
that stirred pots with grace,
now rests... so still.
So light.

Time... is folding in on itself.
It's thick in the room,
like breath held too long.
Like a prayer waiting,
for its own amen.

I hear echoes — soft, familiar.
Gospel songs she used to hum,
when the house was alive,
with Sunday smells,
of her cooking and,
her voice from the kitchen.
Now,
those melodies wrap around me,
like a warm shawl in a cold space.

But the figure on the bed…
she doesn't move.
She doesn't hum.
She doesn't tell me,
everything's going to be alright.

The room is hushed.
Too still.
Like the world stopped spinning,
just for her.

No words.
No sound.
Just breath,
quiet and slow,
feeding the silence.

I want to speak.
To say something.
But all I can do is listen.
To the nothing.
To the everything,
that her stillness holds.

Because right now,
all there is, is this moment.
This room.
This stillness,
I can't put down.

Just… a figure on the bed.
And me, still holding on.

DEMENTIA – WANDERING MIND

"To my mother who suffered Dementia"

Dementia— a word I heard,
but never truly understood,
until it entered our home,
and took you by the hand.

It came softly at first,
like a breeze shifting curtains,
subtle, unseen.
You forgot small things,
a date, a name,
a pot on the stove,
the kettle left to boil.

Once, your thoughts were a sharp thread,
strong, unbroken.
Now they drift
like loose feathers in a storm.
Names blur, faces,
sometimes you search it,
like it's a puzzle you used to know.

You ask - who are you?
if I'm your sister.
Sometimes someone else,
but rarely your daughter.

And yet,
when I hold your hand,
you hold mine back.
Still… Still, somewhere,
you know me.

So, I walk with you,
through this strange, shifting landscape.
No maps. No signs.
Just love as our compass.

Even if your mind wanders far,
I will stay near.
Because love remembers,
what memory forgets.

TO ALL THE MOTHERS IN THE WORLD

To all the mothers near, far and wide,
Who love with hearts they never hide.
Whose hands are worn yet soft and kind,
Whose strength is quiet, deep, refined.

You wake before the morning sun,
Your daily work is never done.
Through sleepless nights and hurried days,
You give your love in countless ways.

With lullabies and guiding hands,
You help us walk, then help us stand.
Through every scrape, through every tear,
You hold us close, you draw us near.

Some birth their own, some choose the role,
Yet all pour out their heart and soul.
In every shape, in every land,
A mother's touch, a gentle hand.

You fight, you heal, you laugh, you cry,
You teach us how to soar and fly.
Your wisdom speaks without a word,
Your silent prayers are always heard.

So, here's to you, the world's bright light,
Who love through day and dream through night.
To all the mothers, strong and true,
The world is better, thanks to you.

A SPECTRUM OF EMOTIONS

Life is a canvas painted with many colours – joy, sorrow, anger, fear, hope, patience, peace, and compassion. This section gathers the emotional threads that weave the human spirit.

ANGER: A CRY FOR HELP

I saw it in his eyes,
before he spoke it,
the tight fists,
the silence after shouting.

He was only a boy,
but the world had already,
been unkind.
His father's anger,
left shadows,
he didn't know how to escape.

The fire inside him,
wasn't rebellion,
it was pain,
bottled up,
from too many nights,
spent afraid.

He didn't want to be angry.
He wanted to be seen,
held, safe.

So, I stayed.
Listened when he couldn't speak.
Loved him through the silence,
through the storm.

And slowly,
he began to heal,
not because the past was gone,
but because he finally knew,
he didn't have to carry it alone.

FRUSTRATION

What is it that twists inside,
when nothing moves the way it should,
not the day,
not the words,
not even the breath you try to take calmly.

Frustration,
is the stillness before the storm,
when you try to explain yourself,
and no one really hears.

It rises,
when you're forced to accept,
what feels unacceptable,
expectations too high,
dreams too far,
the weight of someone else's silence,
when you needed understanding.

Sometimes,
it's the fear that you'll never belong,
or the ache of wanting a life,
you didn't fight hard enough for.

It's not always rage.
Sometimes, it's just a quiet,
folding in of the soul,
a slow disconnection,
from the things you used to believe in.

But in the slow burn,
something shifts.
You begin to see,
frustration is not failure.
It's a signal.
A threshold.
A push toward something deeper,
if you let it speak,
and stay long enough to listen.

CONFUSION

In a world of illusions,
the mind drifts,
uncertain, unanchored.

Each step asks,
where will I land?
The ground shifts,
soft as sinking sand.

Questions scatter,
like autumn leaves,
searching for answers,
that never arrive.

Whispers of thought unravel,
threads loosening in the fog,
drifting away.

Even the stars blur and blend,
their steady light bending,
into unfamiliar paths.

A maze without walls,
without signs,
wandering blind,
through the heart of night.

Yet somewhere ahead,
the faintest glow,
a promise,
that dawn will come.

LOST IN UNCERTAINTY

I linger in limbo, adrift without aim,
Lost in a sea of uncertainty's claim.
The path that once guided, now fades from view,
I'm stranded, bewildered, not sure what to do.

Each day stretches out, like endless expanse,
Yet I'm trapped in the maze, of my own circumstance.
No compass to follow, no map to unfold,
I'm searching for purpose in a story told.

The world spins around me, a whirlwind of pace,
But I'm stuck in a moment frozen in space.
The echoes of purpose once clear in my mind,
Now whispers are muffled hard truths left behind.

Where do I turn when the roads are diverge?
When the flames of ambition begin to submerge.
I'll wait in the silence, embrace the unknown,
For in the stillness, my direction is shown.

Though lost in the shadows, I'll find my own light,
In the depths of confusion, I'll reclaim my sight.
For even in darkness a spark will ignite,
Guiding me forward, through the darkness of night.

So, I'll sit with uncertainty make peace with the doubt,
For in the chaos there's wisdom to sprout.
And though I don't know what tomorrow may bring,
I'll trust in the journey and the song that I'll sing.

COMPASSION

In hearts where kindness finds its home,
Where empathy and love have grown.
There blooms a flower, pure and bright,
A beacon in the darkness night.

Compassion, tender, soft and true,
A force that guides what we must do.
It sees the pain in other's eyes,
And try to make it good and right.

With gentle words and helping hands,
It mends the hurt in distant lands.
A language spoken by the heart,
Uniting us, though worlds apart.

In every soul, a seed resides,
To nurture love that pain divides.
For in compassion, we unite,
And make the world a bit more bright.

PATIENCE

Patience, a whispered word, I often hear,
In moments strained, when tempers flare.
I used to flee, or turn away, pretend,
But now I pause, and try to comprehend.

What is patience? Not just waiting still,
But a quiet strength, against my will.
A softening of the heart, a gentle grace,
To meet harsh words, with a slower pace.

It's in the struggle, the urge to lash out,
That patience grows, a quiet sprout.
A tender seed, nurtured in the soul,
To bear the weight, to make me whole.

I see its power, in goals achieved,
In brighter days, where peace is weaved.
It stills the storm, within my chest,
And guides my choices, for what is best.

God's patient love, a beacon in the night,
Shows me the path, towards the light.
His grace abounds, a constant, gentle rain,
Washing away, my anger and my pain.

So, I breathe deep, and let humility guide,
In troubled times, my steps inside.
For patience learned, is a treasure rare,
A quiet strength, beyond compare.

ANCHORED IN LOVE

Anxiety gathers at the edges of day,
a shadow pressing in,
scattering my spirit,
pulling me off course.

It wraps its fingers around my control,
leaves my body weary,
my soul heavy with ache.

Yet in the quiet,
a whisper rises,
mercy calling through the storm,
reminding me I am held,
in hands of grace.

My heart lifts,
drawn toward a brighter horizon.

Even when shadows tremble,
and storms collide,
I find strength,
not of my own,
but born of faith.

No fear can uproot me,
no sorrow can bind me.
I am anchored,
in love,
in spirit,
in God's abiding presence.

*O Lord, steady my steps,
calm my restless mind.
Let Your light be my compass,
and Your love my home.*

IMAGINATION

Imagination dances, boundless and bright,
In the domain of dreams, where stars ignite.
With whispered tales and shades unseen,
It paints the world in endless sheen.

Through fancied lands, we freely roam,
Where castles rise from thoughts alone.
In skies of blue where clouds take flight,
Imagination fuels our inner light.

With eyes closed tight, we dare to see,
A world of endless possibility.
Where dragons soar and heroes rise,
Imagination holds the keys to skies.

So close your eyes let thoughts take flight,
In scope of wonder, day turns night.
For in the land of dreams we find,
Imagination shapes both heart and mind.

WHY IS LIFE SO COMPLICATED?

Why is life so tangled, Lord?
With paths unclear and truths ignored.
Why must the soul in silence cry?
While questions rise to touch the sky.

You shaped the stars, the breath, the sea,
And yet the life feels a mystery.
A sacred dance of dark and light,
Of trials cloaked in holy night.

We seek the straight, You guide the curve,
And teach through trials what we deserve.
Each burden bears a deeper grace,
Each storm reveals Your hidden face.

In loss, You whisper we're not lost,
In pain, remind us of the cross.
You plant Your peace in deepest ache,
And bloom our hearts each time they break.

For what is life but soul's ascent,
A sacred walk, through firmament?
Though eyes grow dim and flesh may fail,
Your spirit lifts us through the veil.

So let it be, though unrefined,
This tangled thread, divinely lined.
Life's not to solve, but to embrace,
Each step a prayer, each breath Your grace.

FAMILIES, FRIENDS AND RELATIONSHIPS

The bonds we build, nurture, and sometimes lose – family, friendship, and love are at the core of this section. These stories celebrate connection while acknowledging the complexities of relationships.

FAMILY

Family -
a tapestry woven tight,
threads of love,
threads of fight.

We stand,
even when far apart,
hands stretched out,
a beating heart.

But family shifts,
like sand in the wind,
sometimes giving,
sometimes thin.

Laughter cracks to anger,
storms roll in,
and I'm caught,
between the din.

We're pages worn,
a book well-read,
holding love,
and words unsaid.

A mirror deep,
joy and pain collide,
secrets kept,
tears we hide.

Through tangled paths,
I carry this flame,
my family's heart,
my endless name.

MY SIBLINGS

Thirteen hearts, a vibrant beat,
Now eleven remain, their rhythm sweet.
A tapestry of lives, so bright,
Each personality, a guiding light.

Our gatherings, a lively scene,
Where likes and dislikes intertwine.
Beneath the surface, tensions rise,
In clashing wills, and judging eyes.

Never a dull moment, laughter's sound,
With playful jests, the moments abound.
Yet sometimes loud, a boisterous crew,
Each striving, for something new.

The eldest, strong, a guiding hand,
Whose dominance, across the land.
Instilled in the young ones, a quiet fear,
A shadow cast, throughout their young years.

The second, calm, a hidden fire,
Her thoughts concealed, her heart's desire.
The third, observed, a quiet soul,
Misunderstood, beyond control.

The fourth, a preacher, calm and wise,
With reasoned words, and gentle eyes.
The fifth, reserved, a quiet mind,
Until released, his thoughts unwind.

The sixth, discontent, a restless heart,
Yearning for more, a world apart.
The seventh, driven, with opinions strong,
Persistent, striving, righting wrong.

The others' stories, yet untold,
Their paths unique, their spirits bold.
Through quarrels, heartaches, battles won,
A common thread, beneath the sun.

Our faith in Christ, a binding tie,
A love that lifts, and makes us fly.
For future generations, we aspire,
To rise above, and reach higher.

DAUGHTER'S LOVE

Words feel small - how to explain,
what a daughter's love holds?
In her laughter, a melody soft and clear,
a song that lingers, pure and whole.

Her eyes sparkle at the smallest gift,
thoughtful in ways,
that never ask for much.

In her dreams, worlds unfold,
vast and bright - held gently,
in a mother's heart.

Through every joy,
through every tear,
a daughter's love stays close,
steady and near.

Her smile - a light that stretches
far beyond the day,
a quiet happiness
that moves in miles.

Life's road is never easy,
twists and turns come fast,
but she learns to wear a smile,
never letting sorrow last.

Friends and family, near and far,
shine like stars around her path.

Faces flicker, places blend,
snapshots of colour,
trying to find their place.

From morning light,
to evening's sigh,
she wonders - what next?

And still, the story flows,
a daughter's love, always held,
always valued.

A DAUGHTER'S JOURNEY

From shadowed past, a spirit bright,
Across the years, where shadows hide.
My daughter's life, a tapestry of light,
With darkness woven, side by side.

In parks we picnicked, laughter's gleam,
With brothers playing, by the stream.
Mount Maunganui's sun-kissed shore,
Creating memories, to explore.

Through school camps, movies, fleeting years,
Grandparents' love, dispelling fears.
Her spirit soared, though shadows fell,
A heart of gold, she knew so well.

And now she stands, with grace and might,
Her spirit stronger, shining bright.
My friend, my daughter, wise and true,
My rock, my confidante, anew.

Beyond the silence, deep and true,
Reveals a spirit, forged anew.
In quiet strength, her journey's shown,
A life transformed, a heart that's grown.

GOD SEES YOU, SON

You walk in silence, strong and still,
A quiet soul with iron will.
Your love runs deep, though words are few,
A steady heart, so fierce, so true.

You've faced the dark, the storms, the fight,
But held your ground without the light.
You love your kids with all you are,
Still feel you're reaching for the stars.

But son, the Lord has seen each tear,
He's walked beside you, always near.
No need to carry this alone,
Just speak His name, and you'll be known.

He knows your heart beneath the pain,
And offers rest, like gentle rain.
Believe, and ask – He's at your side,
With open arms and love that won't hide.

A STEADY FLAME

My second son, with a steadfast heart,
You've stood your ground, played every part.
A loving soul, a faithful friend,
With strength and truth that never bend.

Like your siblings, you love with might,
A caring father, firm and kind.
You pour your heart, mind and soul,
To plant the seeds to help them grow.

In tools or boots, you give your all,
On fields of play or when walls fall.
A builder of dreams with hands that shape,
No task too hard, no form too great.

You journeyed far through storm and flame,
Yet held your hope, stayed in the game.
And now you've found what few can say,
A love that's real, that's here to stay.

I see the road you chose,
The ups and downs, the highs and lows.
Forever proud of all you've done,
A loyal friend and loving son.

TWO HALVES OF A WHOLE

Born together, yet worlds apart,
Two souls bound by a single start.
Older, clever, a sneaky mind,
A master of mischief, the tricky kind.

Younger, quiet, a shadow near,
Gentle and shy, but always here.
Clinging close in a world unknown,
Finding comfort in the bond they've grown.

One spins webs of wit and guile,
A daring grin, a devilish smile.
The other watches, soft and still,
A heart that bends but holds its will.

Together they dance, a complex tune,
One a spark, the other a moon.
Opposing forces, yet deeply tied,
A bind no difference could divide.

Though paths may turn, their hearts align,
Two fraternal twins, a love divine.
For in their differences, a truth is clear,
Opposites thrive when bound by care.

MY NIECE – THE DOCTOR

A dream once whispered, now fulfilled,
With knowledge honed and strength instilled.
Through sleepless nights and test endured,
Your heart stayed steadfast; your path assured.

In halls of healing, where hope abides,
You walk with wisdom as your guide.
Each patient's story, a trust bestowed,
Each life you touch, a kindness showed.

White coat draped, a badge of care,
A healer's spirit, strong and rare.
From stethoscope to healing art,
You mend the body, soothe the heart.

We celebrate the path you've trod,
Your dedication, a gift from God.
To be a doctor is more than a role,
It's a calling that springs from a giving soul.

So, here's to you, niece, with endless pride,
With love and joy that cannot hide.
The world is brighter with what you do,
A doctor, a miracle, and always you.

FRIENDSHIP

In the garden of life, where flowers bloom,
There exists a bond, beyond any gloom.
Friendship, a treasure, pure and true,
Like a guiding star, always in view.

Through laughter and tears, hand in hand,
Together we walk, a united band.
In moments of joy or times of despair,
A friend's presence, a solace rare.

With words unspoken, they understand,
A connection so deep, like grains of sand.
In the tapestry of life, they weave a thread,
Binding hearts together, where love is spread.

Friendship, a melody, sweet and clear,
A symphony of trust, devoid of fear.
In the book of memories, they pen a tale,
Of companionship strong, beyond any gale.

So cherish each friend, hold them near,
For in the journey of life, they bring cheer.
Like a beacon of light, in the darkest night,
shines bright, a guiding light.

THE OCEAN IN HIS EYES

He came into the world,
bright as morning light,
a boy full of laughter,
drawn to water like breath to air.

The sea was his song,
the pool, his playground.
Summer wrapped around him,
like a second skin.

But time shifted.
His feet grew restless.
His thoughts scattered,
always moving,
always reaching.

They call it ADHD.
A mind that runs ahead,
never quite still.

He finds quiet in a phone screen,
connection in his own rhythm.
And I watch,
loving him deeply,
even when I don't understand.

Still, I see him,
that boy,
with the ocean in his eyes.

So, I walk beside him,
with patience,
with grace.
Because he is my grandson,
and every part of him,
is a gift.

THROUGH THE EYES OF A CHILD, WHEN NOBODY WAS LOOKING

Nobody was looking,
When 8 to 10 years olds were taken.
Presented to court without any legal representation.
Then to State Care Institutions,
Where they stayed until they found a solution.

Nobody was looking,
When police randomly picked us up.
From the streets or in the clubs,
Taken to prison for no apparent reason.
Locked in the cell with revolting smell,
It was a place from hell.

Nothing made any sense,
As they had taken everything away.
But I know that I would give anything,
To stand up on my feet one day.

Sadness was the feeling,
When the falling didn't stop.
It stripped away my life meaning,
And all the good things that I got.

When I finally hit rock bottom,
And I looked back up at the sky.
What I once had, seems so far away,
The only thing left to do was cry.

Why was I tortured like this?
I did not do anyone any wrong.
All I wanted was to understand,
And to ask for a helping hand.
WHEN NOBODY WAS LOOKING

A WONDERFUL BLESSING

The night was long, the hours slow,
A waiting heart, a hopeful glow.
Through whispered prayers and weary sighs,
We longed to gaze in newborn eyes.

The world stood still, the time felt vast,
But then-at last, at last, at last.
A cry so pure, so soft, so sweet,
A tiny soul, our joy complete.

Sunday's dawn, a gift so bright,
Wrapped in love, bathed in light.
The pain dissolved, the tears ran free,
For now, dear child, we hold thee.

My sister's first grandchild, a love so new,
A blessing rare, a dream come true.
Thanks be to God for this perfect grace,
His love shines bright in your tiny face.

GRIEF AND HEALING

Grief is both a weight and a teacher. This section walks through the valleys of loss, but also toward the slow light of healing and renewal.

IF ONLY

"The day my husband passed–30/01/2014"
If only I hadn't gone to work that day,
maybe the story would've ended differently.
But it was my last shift,
before a long-awaited break.

Still, I think back,
what if I had returned,
just to grab the snack I'd forgotten?
What if I hadn't rushed,
to catch that bus,
or buy that ticket?

If only I hadn't waited,
for a call that never came.
If only I had listened,
to that quiet warning inside,
something felt wrong,
I had a choice.

If only I had gone home,
the moment he stopped answering.
If only I hadn't waited.
If only I got there in time.

But time didn't wait for me.
He left,
without a word,
without goodbye.

Ten years on,
and the ache still breathes
in the silence of that day.

All I can say is,
"If only..."
But no whisper of regret,
can rewrite the ending.

FOR HER WHO FOUGHT SO LONG

"In memory of my sister-in-law Faleulu Collins-Alapati"

She walked through life with quiet grace,
A warmth, a light, in every space.
A sister's laughter, wife's embrace,
A mother's love, time can't erase.

Through days of illness, pain held tight,
She bore it all, with fierce soft might.
In every struggle, every tear,
She showed us love, and hope appear.

Her hands, though tired still held ours,
Through sleepless nights and passing hours.
In whispered words, in softened sigh,
She gave us strength as she grew wise.

Now gentle peace is hers to keep,
She's free from pain, in endless sleep.
Yet in our hearts she still remains,
A part of us, through joy and pain.

Remember her, not in her fight,
But in her love, her boundless light.
For every moment, that she gave,
Lives on in us, her spirit saved.

A DECADE WITHOUT YOU, DAD

Dad's passing, 9th Feb 2015 - 10th years anniversary 2025

Ten years have passed yet you stay,
In every thought, in every way.
A guiding light, though out of sight,
Your love still shined forever bright.

You taught us strength with firm kind hands,
Worked the fields and fished the lands.
Through sun and storm, through calm and tide,
For family's sake you stood with pride.

A man of faith, you knelt to pray,
Trusting God to lead the way.
Your wisdom shaped the lives you touched,
Your presence, oh, we miss so much.

The sea still calls, the earth still grows,
But life without you ebbs and flows.
Though time moves on, our hearts remain,
Forever blessed to bear your name.

Rest in peace, dear Dad, above,
Wrapped in God's unending love.

FOR OUR FIFTH AT THE TABLE

In memory of a friend and colleague who had moved on

There once were five at every meet,
A circle close, a bond so sweet.
Through laughter, meals, and moments rare,
One gentle soul lit up the air.

She walked through storms with quiet grace,
No pain betrayed upon her face.
For many years, yet still she smiled,
A strength so pure, so soft, so mild.

She never missed a photo's snap,
A captured time, a heartfelt map.
Of friendships deep, of love so true,
Of memories made with all of you.

Now four remain to share the day,
Yet in our hearts, she's never away.
For every laugh and every cheer,
We feel her presence lingering near.

We meet, we chat, we dine, we share,
And sometimes forget the photo there.
But know she sees, from skies above,
Still part of every meal and love.

So raise a glass, and toast her name,
For in our hearts, she stays the same.
Our fifth in spirit, soft and bright---
A star that shines in ladies' night.

WHEN STILLNESS HEALS

Birdsong drifts,
soft, steady,
a rhythm that rocks the world quiet.

The sun rests on my skin,
warm and unhurried.
Here, in this stillness,
I find space to simply be.

With eyes closed,
I slip into memory,
laughter echoing through trees,
bare feet chasing shadows,
in sun-drenched woods.

There were no burdens then.
Only wind, light,
and the steady pull of joy.

Now,
this silence holds me,
It listens. It heals.

Worn thoughts settle,
tears retreat.
Fear softens its grip.

I return not unchanged,
but steadier,
Clearer.
Held by something deeper.

The world is still the same,
But I see it now.
with eyes that have rested,
and a heart,
that remembers,
how to breathe.

FRUIT OF THE TONGUE

A whisper can wound, a word can heal.
The tongue holds power no hand can feel.
With syllables soft or daggers sharp,
It shapes the soul, it stirs the heart.

It speaks of death – it plants despair,
Or breathes out life, like sweetest air.
A curse can crush, a lie can bind,
But truth and love can free the mind.

Each word we sow, we one day reap,
In joy's bright light or sorrow deep.
So speak with care, with grace and might,
Let voices bloom with hope and light.

For those who love to speak will see,
The fruit they grow on word-born tree.
So may our tongues sow seeds of peace,
And bring to life a world's release.

THE ECHO OF MY HEALING

There was a time I wore a smile,
To hide the storm, to cope awhile.
Behind closed doors, my spirit cried,
A quiet voice I pushed aside.

I gave my all, I played the part,
A young bride with a hopeful heart.
But love, I learned, can wear disguise,
A cage behind familiar eyes.

I walked through years of fractured grace,
His shadow lingering in my space.
Even work, my only shield,
Was pierced by pain I couldn't yield.

But silence doesn't mean defeat,
The soul remembers how to beat.
From broken vows, I found my flame,
A softer strength, a louder name.

Today, I breathe without regret,
My past still echoes, but with less threat.
For in the silence, I became whole,
This is the healing of my soul.

WORK LIFE BALANCE

Here are the reflections of a life lived between duty and passion, responsibility and rest. It is about the lessons learned in trying to balance work, family, and self. It also marks the end of an era - stepping into retirement, a season of change that brings both relief and uncertainty. This section reflects on how one copes with letting go of long-held roles, finding new rhythms, and embracing life beyond work with grace and resilience.

KEEPING BUSY

In the hum of life,
we find our rhythm,
each day unfolding,
from dawn's soft light,
to evening's quiet sigh.

The world moves quickly.
Footsteps echo on pavement,
voices blur in meetings,
emails stack like bricks.
Still, we move— hands steady,
hearts somewhere in the doing.

We craft our hours,
with checklists and calls,
errands and dinners,
folding small moments
into the rush.

Even in chaos,
we search for balance,
a pause in the noise,
a breath in the middle,
of everything.

Our minds, like rivers,
never still,
always reaching,
dreaming, building.

And somewhere,
between task and thought,
we find meaning.
Not in the rush itself,
but in the rhythm,
that keeps us going.

LEARNING ANOTHER TONGUE

A new tongue, a new world to explore,
Though age may weigh, I crave still more.
My learning days, far from their end,
In Te Reo's embrace, I transcend.

My curiosity, a guiding light,
Illuminates the path, both dark and bright.
To understand the dialects' art,
Each nuance, a new beat to my heart.

Te Reo's levels, one and two,
A daunting task, yet I see it through.
I isolate myself, a conscious choice,
From mother tongue, a different voice.

The alphabet song, a playful test,
Each syllable, a challenge to digest.
Some words echo Samoan's sound,
Yet Māori's rhythm, must be found.

Pronunciation's dance, a tricky game,
To speak with grace, and avoid all shame.
I listen closely to podcasts' flow,
Te Reo's music, starts to grow.

Respect and grace, my guiding star,
To learn with care, and go so far.
This journey's worth, beyond compare,
A new voice found, beyond despair.

SIDE BY SIDE – A MOMENT IN TIME

She drove like she owned the streets,
confident hands, music low,
weaving through traffic,
with a calm that made me nervous.

Sunlight blinked through trees,
shadows flickered across the dash.
I sat quietly,
half in awe,
half bracing for impact.

The city rushed by,
horns, people,
the scent of coffee and urgency.
She found a parking spot,
like it was waiting for her all along.

Inside the café,
I opened my notebook,
but the words stayed still.

She sat across from me,
stirring her drink,
completely at ease.

And in that moment,
I realized,
this was the story.

Sometimes,
the journey is louder,
than the destination.
And sometimes,
if you are lucky,
your daughter is the one,
driving you there.

EMERGENCY

The clock struck two,
a chill in the bones,
as we sped through sleeping streets,
uphill, downhill,
chasing answers in the dark.

The Emergency Room,
crowded, loud,
forms in hand,
fear in my chest.

People lined the walls,
some on stretchers,
some on the floor.
Voices clashed,
machines beeped,
hope flickered.

Through swinging doors,
a battlefield of beds.
No space.
No silence.
Just motion.

Porters moved with grace,
carving paths in chaos.

Finally, a doctor - calm, clear.
"Not good, but not the worst."

Pain relief.
Fluids. Tests.
Still waiting.

Fifteen hours later,
we were released.
Not fixed. Just done.

The system groaned behind us,
a promise,
it couldn't quite keep.

FEELING SICK

A devotional reflection
Lord,
we live as if each breath,
is ours to command,
forgetting how fragile we are,
until sickness reminds us,
we are dust,
held together by Your grace.

When the fever comes,
when the body aches,
and strength slips quietly away,
we remember:
we are not in control.

But You are.

In the stillness of pain,
You speak.
Not in thunder,
but in the hush,
between heartbeats.
Be still,
and know that I am God.

This suffering, though heavy,
draws us near.
It peels back pride,
softens our hearts,
and opens our hands,
to receive what we cannot earn:
Your peace.
Your presence.
Your healing,
in body and in soul.

Even here, Lord,
especially here,
we find You.

END OF AN ERA

Today,
I stand at the edge of a chapter closing.
Not with regret— but with reflection.
Not with fanfare— but with quiet pride.

Years in public service have shaped me,
through policy and people,
deadlines and decisions,
early mornings and long, silent nights,
that few ever saw.

I gave my best,
and sometimes more than I had.
I stayed when it was hard to stay.
I spoke up,
when silence would have been easier.
And I found meaning,
in moments no one clapped for.

We completed projects, hit targets,
navigated the shifting winds of leadership,
and change.
Some things worked.
Others did not.
But always,
I showed up—with integrity.

Redundancy came suddenly,
and yes, it is hard.
But it also invites reflection,
and space for something new.

To my colleagues,
you were not just co-workers.
You were comrades.
Soul-holders on the tough days.
Thank you for the laughter,
the honesty, the shared victories
and even the hard conversations.

To my family and closest friends,
your patience was quiet,
but never unnoticed.
You made sacrifices so I could serve.
You carried me in ways
I could never repay.

And now,
as I close this chapter,
I carry more than just experience.
I carry perspective,
resilience,
and relationships
that do not end here.

So, I leave with a full heart,
not because it was easy,
but because it mattered.

This chapter ends.
And I walk forward,
tearful, grateful,
and wide open,
to what comes next.

Thank you.

RETIREMENT

The clock slows – at last, it's here,
The workday's hum has disappeared.
No rush, no deadlines drawing near,
The weight is gone, the path is clear.

The sun now shines in gentler hue,
The world feels wide, the hours new.
Each morning starts with quiet grace,
An open heart, a softened pace.

The days expand, the moments stay,
No need to chase, no need to sway.
Dreams once hidden, pressed away,
Now rise and bloom in bright display.

So, here's to me, my journey bright,
To tender dusk and starlit night.
For in this time my spirit's free,
A life to savour endlessly.

MY QUIET FIRE

The house is still, no clocks chime,
No deadlines press, just open time.
I miss the pulse of working days,
The sharpened mind, the winding maze.

I've wandered through this slower pace,
A softer life, an open space.
Yet often in the hush I find,
A restless heart, an untamed mind.

I turned to keys, the piano's song,
To soothe the hours, to feel I belong.
The notes began, a gentle start,
A spark returned, a quickened heart.

But once it passed, the stillness came,
The mind unlit, the self the same.
Then whispers rose, both stern and kind:
*"You've faced the storm, yet still you climb,
Through loss, through pain, you've walked before,
You can begin and rise once more."*

So I will move, not rushed, but true,
Seek out the fresh, embrace the new.
A deeper song, a brighter flame,
A life that's rich beyond a name.

For meaning hides in quiet things,
In keys that play, in thoughts that sing.
And though the fire may fade or tire,
I'll always climb a little higher.

MORNING WORKOUT

The alarm rings,
not loud, just persistent.
Like doubt.
Like that voice that says,
Why bother today?

Still, I get up.
Lace my shoes.
It feels like something small,
but it isn't.

Outside, the world is still.
No traffic yet, no emails,
no one asking anything of me.
Just me, and this promise I've made,
to show up for myself.

Each step hurts.
My breath catches.
But I move through it,
not to be perfect, just to begin.

The air is cold against my face.
My lungs protest.
But the rhythm comes.
And so does clarity.

The sun rises slowly,
not dramatic, but steady.
And I like to think it sees me.
Sees the fight.
The choosing.
The becoming.

This is my space,
before the world makes its demands.
This is where I remind myself,
I am stronger than yesterday,
even if only by a little.

And that is enough.

NATURE AND INSPIRATION

In the stillness of nature, inspiration flows freely. This section honours the earth, sky, sea, and all the beauty that reminds us of life's wonder and sacredness.

HEAVEN'S MORNING LIGHT

The morning sun slips,
through the clouds,
not loud,
just soft enough to wake the soul.
Its golden warmth rests on my skin,
quietly saying:
Begin again.

I lift my gaze,
to the wide, open sky,
and feel the hush of His presence.
Every ray,
a gentle reminder.
Every breeze,
a whispered prayer.
I am here.

The night has passed.
Whatever came before,
now falls behind.
His mercy meets me,
with the light,
new,
unchanging,
always near.

I don't know what today will hold.
But I walk into it,
not alone.

With faith in one hand,
and grace in the other,
I take the next step.

The sun,
the sky,
the stillness of morning,
all echo one truth:
God is only ever
a breath away.

SUNDAY MORNING

The living room is quiet,
sunlight soft and dim,
"Lord, I need You,"
plays, a comforting hymn.
It's Sunday morning,
a time for soul to rest,
To let the worries fade,
and put my heart to test.

The hills are shrouded,
in a misty, grey embrace,
The wind whispers gently,
in this peaceful, sacred space.
This precious time,
a gift I hold so dear,
To think of loved ones,
and banish every fear.

The melody's sweet sound,
a balm upon my heart,
A reminder of His love,
right from the very start.
This Sunday morning,
a chance to start anew,
With gratitude and hope,
and faith that sees me through.

BEAUTIFUL DAY

What a beautiful day,
the bay opens wide,
its calm waters holding the sky,
like a mirror of light.

Birds wheel and glide,
their wings catching the breeze,
seagulls calling above,
as if singing to the sea.

Not a cloud drifts by,
only the silver gleam of planes,
sliding quietly overhead.

I sit in the warmth of the sun,
soaking in the stillness,
watching joggers trace,
their steady paths along the shore.

Children laugh across the field,
their voices carrying like bells.
Dogs tumble in circles,
tails wagging faster than time,
the world alive in their play.

Oh, what a beautiful day,
waves move slowly,
like the earth breathing,
all around the bay.

And in this gentle rhythm,
I feel the sacred nearness of life,
a quiet prayer rising,
a reminder that beauty itself,
is a blessing,

and gratitude the truest song,
of the soul.

NATURE'S BEAUTY

Behind my parents' house,
I sit. I listen.
Buzzing. Clicking.
A pulse beneath the air.

Insects flicker in the heat.
The hum of life is constant,
but never loud enough to drown the city.

Just beyond - streets bustle.
Cars move like rivers.
People rush like wind.
Their footsteps, their voices,
a beat - a rhythm always rising.

But above it all,
birds cut through the sky with ease.
They sing without rush, without fear.
Their melody doesn't ask for permission.

The sun glides overhead,
catching rooftops, warming skin.
Everything glows.
Everything breathes.

Blue sky - open, endless,
watching as life unfolds below.

And me? I'm just here.
Still. Quiet.
Witnessing.

Because even in the chaos,
even in the noise - nature speaks.
Soft. True. Unshaken.

And if I listen, really listen...
I remember,
there's beauty everywhere.
Even here. Even now.
Even in the middle of it all.

NATURE'S PAINTING HUNG

Upon the wall a painting rests,
houses clustered by the sea,
mountains rising in silent grace,
roads winding gently,
through a tranquil space.

But lean closer,
and the canvas opens wide.
Step through the frame,
suddenly you are there.

The salt of the sea,
meets the breath of the pines.
Waves brush the shore,
like a hand smoothing stone.
Mountains stand eternal,
their silence steady,
their shadows cool.

Trees sway,
their branches whispering songs,
the wind has carried for centuries.
A path curves ahead,
inviting your feet,
to wander without hurry.

So let it hang upon the wall,
a doorway waiting,
a portal to peace,
where sea and mountain,
meet in harmony,
and the soul remembers,
its home.

THE VIEW I KEEP

Each morning,
I pause at the window,
a moment carved out,
of routine and restlessness.

Greenery stretches beyond the glass,
soft, familiar, wrapped in calm.
A low stone wall stands steady,
weathered by seasons,
but still holding its place,
like an old friend who never left.

The walkway just outside,
brings people I'll never meet,
passing shadows,
fragments of lives in motion.

Now and then, a fluffy grey cat appears,
shoulders low, tail flicking with purpose.
She's hunting,
maybe rats, maybe ghosts,
and I root for her,
like I would for a childhood hero.

Birds dart through the trees,
brilliant and bold, filling the air,
with songs I didn't know I missed,
until I heard them again.

Winter has crept in,
not cruel, just colder,
with wind that howls
around the corners of the house,
like it's looking for a way in.

And still, outside my window,
life continues,
quiet, ordinary,
beautiful in its own way.

SOUND OF RAIN

The rain began, a soft and gentle plea,
Awakening me, at six, to what I see.
Not just raindrops falling, but a sweet embrace,
A soothing comfort, in this quiet, sacred space.

The rhythm of the rain, a comfort to my soul,
A gentle healing, making me feel whole.
It whispers secrets, only rain can know,
Of peace and solace, in this gentle, steady flow.

Silver threads descend from heavens high above,
Weaving tales of peace, and gentle, quiet love.
A symphony of rain, a liquid, silver stream,
Washing away the worries, like a fading, distant dream.

MORNING'S STILLNESS

I sit within my cozy chair,
The morning paints the softest air.
The sun peeks through the clouds of grey,
Then slowly, gently fades away.

The world is hushed, the streets still sleep,
While golden light begins to seep.
The only sound – the birds that sing,
Or softly to each other cling.

The voices weave the quiet air,
A tender song beyond compare.
And in this still and sacred hour,
I feel the hush, the hope, the power.

TIME

Time —
a river that never pauses,
moving swift and deep.

It offers itself freely,
whether we notice or not.
Waking or sleeping,
it flows. Constant.
Silent. Irreplaceable.

We try to hold it,
but it slips through our fingers,
like sand too fine to grasp.

It is both gift and burden,
companion and challenge.
A double-edged presence,
that carries our laughter,
and our grief in equal measure.

It does not wait.
It does not bend.
But it marks us,
from our first breath to our last.

Each second a thread,
in the fabric of who we are.
Gone before we name it.

And still - we chase it.
We fear it.
We long for more of it.

Time: not just a ticking clock,
but the shape of our being.
A quiet teacher, a mirror,
a truth.

And I - I am simply a soul,
passing through,
its current.

TIME: THE PRICELESS THREAD

Time is not a coin we spend,
Nor treasure stored that wealth can lend.
It is moments wrapped in breath and light,
The hush between each day and night.

It's not the ticking of a clock,
But memories etched of life's own rock.
A baby's cry, a mother's smile,
A journey walked through every mile.

It cannot pause, it will not bend,
It flows from start to silent end.
No power halts its quiet flight,
It slips through fingers, soft as night.

So spend it well on love and grace,
Not chasing fame or fruitless race.
For time, once gone, won't turn around,
Its worth is deep, its voice profound.

It is the thread in every seam,
The weaver of each hope and dream.

BEFORE IT SLIPS AWAY

We count the hours,
chase the day,
yet miss the moments
that softly sway,
a glance, a laugh,
a word unsaid,
while thoughts keep racing
far ahead.

We trade our time,
for goals and pride,
but something hollows,
deep inside.

"I'll make time," we say,
but it drifts, quietly,
like evening mist.

And the truth,
often found too late:
time won't rewind.
It will not wait.

So…
hold the ones,
who hold your name,
speak the truth,
without the shame.

Let each hour,
carry grace,
and find your soul,
in its own place.

Because life is made,
of moments small,
and choosing love,
might be the greatest,
choice of all.

SNAPSHOTS OF LIFE, LEISURE & ADVENTURE

Life is more than a struggle – it is also play, laughter, discovery, and adventure. These snapshots capture the lighter, freer moments that bring balance and joy.

TRINKETS BOX

A weathered pine box,
rough and familiar,
sits quietly on the dresser.

Its light brown frame,
faded by time,
striped with green,
that only sunlight reveals.

Once polished and bright,
now dimmed,
a keeper of small treasures.

A necklace tree leans,
rings lie still,
echoes of hands,
that once played here.

Inside, soft red cloth,
cradles old things:
bangles, pins,
a broken brooch,
a ballerina,
who no longer twirls.

Childhood ended her dance,
but not the story.
The music has faded,
but memory remains.

The trinket box,
sitting quietly,
waiting,
for someone to remember,
what once was loved.

PAINTING ON THE WALL

There's a painting above my bed,
a creamy frame,
gold-lined and soft.
I look at it each day,
drawn into its quiet world.

Blue waters stretch,
beneath drifting boats,
clouds mirrored in their calm.
A lighthouse stands watch,
while hills and homes lean,
gently into the breeze.

A garden blooms,
a path winds through stillness,
and a single tree rises,
steadfast and simple.

From afar,
it's just a picture.
Up close,
it feels like memory.
Peace stitched,
into every brushstroke.

I wonder sometimes,
is it a place out there,
or
just a quiet part of me?

A MATTER OF MERIT

We stood in line,
quiet, steady, unshaken.
Not loud in fashion,
or dripping wealth,
but grounded in who we are.

Our skin, brown.
Our clothes, simple.
And yet,
your glance said more,
than your words.

"This is first,"
you said - certain,
without a second thought,
without looking at a single ticket.

Just assumption,
thinly veiled,
as authority.

But we belong.
Not just in these seats,
but in every space,
we've fought to stand.

We've earned our place,
through more than miles,
through patience,
through grace,
through rising,
in the face of being told we couldn't.

Next time,
before you measure worth,
by what's worn,
or what's assumed,
remember: First class,
is not always dressed in gold.

Sometimes, it walks in quietly.
And today, it was me.

SUBMERGED IN SERENITY

In silence, I descend through liquid skies,
Where sunlight dances, then slowly dies.
The world above fades, a fleeting dream,
As I sink into the ocean's gleam.

Around me, a ballet of colours unfolds,
Fishes in hues of silver and gold.
Angelfish gliding, their fins like wings,
Butterfly fish weaving delicate rings.

Seaweeds sway in the gentle tide,
Hiding shy creatures that choose to bide.
I stretch out my hands, a playful caress,
And feel the pulse of life in their finesse.

Deeper I dive, where the shadows creep,
Where secrets are cradled in waters deep.
My feet brush the seabed, soft and cool,
A realm unspoiled, serene and full.

In this watery world, I am weightless, free,
A child of the waves, cradled by the sea.
With every breath, I'm alive, reborn,
In the deep embrace of the ocean's moon.

FREEFALL THRILLS

Strapped together, hearts aligned,
We soared beyond the earth confined.
The plane's roar faded, a distant hum,
As the edge of the world dared us to come.

The door swung wide; the rush began,
A leap of faith, no solid land.
The wind screamed loud, a wild refrain,
Freedom running through every vein.

Weightless, spinning, the earth drew near,
A mixture of thrill and fear.
Time stretched thin in that brief dive,
The purest moment of being alive.

Then, a tug – the parachute bloomed,
The frantic fall became attuned.
We floated now, soothing glide,
Above the world, with nothing to hide.

The sky embraced us, vast and blue,
A fleeting bond, just me and you.
From freefall's thrill to the gentle descent,
A memory made, a life well-spent.

TO MILFORD SOUND, BEFORE THE DAWN

We left before the world awoke,
When morning wore its velvet cloak.
The stars still hung in silent grace,
As we set forth to nature's place.

A breath of chill, the breeze so light,
Wrapped gently round the fading night.
Then slowly came the soft sunrise,
A golden wash across the skies.

We paused to catch each perfect view,
Where lakes lay still, and mountains grew.
At Mirror Lake, the world stood twin,
Reflections deep, like peace within.

The ridges rose in ancient pride,
With waterfalls that danced and cried.
We marvelled at each tumbling stream,
Like whispers woven through a dream.

By midday, down the path we came,
To where the water knew no name.
A boat awaited, still and proud,
To take us where the skies touch cloud.

Into the Sound we gently glided,
By cliffs and crests the sea divided.
Waterfalls fell from heights untold,
Like silver threads through green and gold.

Mountains stood like watchful kings,
Wrapped in mist with eagle wings.
And all around, a hush so deep,
It stirred the soul, it made it weep.

We watched, we breathed, we held the grace,
Of Milford Sound, that sacred place.
Where earth and heaven seem to meet,
And leave their silence at our feet.

A journey made, a memory sown,
In nature's arms, we were alone.
But never more completely found,
Than in the heart, of Milford Sound.

ZIPLINING THROUGH THE WILD

Harness snug, helmet tight,
Eyes wide open, pure delight.
She giggled loud, "Are you afraid?"
I laughed, "No – I'm brave today."

Strapped in tight, we leap from the ledge,
Granddaughter's grin wide at the edge.
The world drops fast, the river roars,
Adventure calls from forest floors.

She squealed with joy, arms open wide,
We slice the wind like birds flying.
Below, the water twists and shines,
A silver serpent of ancient lines.

Through valleys green and mountain air,
We found a thrill no words could share.
Not just the rush, not just the flight,
But holding close a moment's light.

At last, we stopped, feet on the ground,
Still tingling from that soaring sound.
With love, with laughter, side by side,
And hearts that leap, and zip, and glide.

MY GET AWAY CARD

Sixty-five approaching,
and I needed out.
Not a party, not a fuss.
Just space.
A quiet escape, mine alone.

Flights booked. Hotel chosen.
A map of freedom folded in my pocket.
I told no one.
Silence became my safety.

But my daughter knew.
Her eyes understood.
Her heart held the secret,
for a while.
Then it unravelled.

My sisters found out.
The silent unravelled into laughter,
questions, plans.

And suddenly,
paradise wasn't mine alone,
it was ours.

Their joy,
cracked open something in me.
"Why not?" I said - a whisper,
through rising tears.

Worry lingered,
would it be too much?
Too late?

But beneath it, hope stirred.
A first.
A chance to connect again,
not as we were, but as we are now.
Two weeks ahead.
And maybe, this time,
It will be alright.

JETBOATING WITH THE FAMILY

We buckle in tight, hearts on the rise,
The river ahead under big open skies.
The engine roars loud, like a lion at play,
Adventure is calling – no turning away.

Spray on our faces, wind in our hair,
Laughter exploding, flying through air.
We twist and turn with a wild, sharp spin,
A scream then a giggle, from deep down within.

I hold on tight, son's wide with a grin,
The grandson shouts "Again" with a joy from within.
Water like silver, sunlight like gold,
These are the memories we'll keep when we're old.

We skim past the rocks, we dash under bridges,
Each splash is a cheer, each wave feels like drift.
Together we soar, on water's fast track,
No worries ahead and no looking back.

Jetboating moments – so fierce and so free,
A family adventure, wild as can be.
Not just a ride, but a bond that will last,
Written in laughter and splashes that passed.

WINGS ABOVE THE WATER

A low hum the boat - glides forward,
slicing the sea with quiet purpose.

Waves shimmer,
trailing behind in soft applause,
as we drift toward the horizon,
where everything feels possible.

The harness pulls firm.
The parachute blooms,
a sudden bloom of colour,
against the wind.

And then - we rise.
The ocean drops away,
the boat becomes a whisper,
and the sky claims us.

Below, the water glows deep sapphire,
edges frosted with foam.
The city spreads out like scattered thoughts,
while hills hold still,
beneath the quiet promise,
of morning light.

Up here, the wind speaks,
in a language we don't need to translate.
It tells stories only the air remembers.

The view is more than beauty,
it's breathless belonging.
Sea and skyline, man and nature,
briefly in balance.

From below, the boat calls us back.
But for now, we hover,
suspended between worlds.

And when we begin to descend,
it's the spirit that stays aloft.
Because once you've touched,
the hush of sky, everything below,
feels changed.

SUITCASE STORIES

Another island.
Another chance to begin again.
I came alone - a suitcase in hand,
but carrying far more than clothes.

Memories folded tight,
goodbyes that still echo,
and a silence,
from those who never asked,
why I had to leave.
No itinerary.
No final plans.
Only the pull,
to somewhere I could breathe.

The plane lifted, and for once,
my body didn't flinch.
No racing thoughts,
no clenched jaw - just sky,
and the quiet ache of release.

The hours passed in a soft blur,
the kind that comes,
after too many nights,
without sleep.
And then - his voice: the pilot,
gentle, grounding.
The descent was steady.
The earth waited.
I braced for nothing,
and found peace instead.

A breath exhaled.
Not victory, but survival.

And as the wheels met land,
I knew: this arrival,
was more than physical.
It was the first time,
I didn't want to run.

DISORIENTING ARRIVAL

Dropped into darkness,
no bearings, no reason,
just the hum of machines,
and the sterile breath,
of nowhere.

Corridors bent like illusions.
Doors repeated themselves.
Nothing made sense.
Everything watched.

I chased numbers,
that slipped away.
Up. Down.
Again and Again.
Still lost.

The walls closed in.
No voices. No light.
Only the echo of my own unrest.

Then…
a crack in the silence.
A narrow way.
I pushed through.

Found it.
Not safety.
Just an end,
to the spiral.

The room waited,
still and dim.
And I stood there,
heart pounding,
like I'd survived,
something unnamed.

LOVE, HAPPINESS, AND THANKS

This closing section is a song of gratitude, celebrating love in its many forms and giving thanks for life's blessings, both big and small. It also embraces the transition into retirement, a time to pause and cherish what has been achieved while discovering joy in new beginnings. Here, love and happiness are not just memories, but guiding lights for the days yet to come.

LOVE

What is love,
if not a glimpse of the divine,
a quiet strength,
a flame that never fades?

Scripture tells us,
God is *love*,
not far off, but here,
steady and sure.

We see it in beauty,
in the sea, the sky,
the kindness we give,
and receive.

His love reaches all,
broken, whole,
seeking, lost.
Not because we deserve it,
but because He is love.

When fear surrounds you,
and shadows press in,
lean into that love,
not just in prayer,
but in the way you live.

So let it live in you,
in your words,
your mercy,
your daily grace.

Love is the gift,
and the call.

GOODNESS OF GOD

Morning breaks,
a chill in the air,
and the week waits ahead.

Then the song begins,
"The Goodness of God"
and I remember.

His love finds me,
even when I drift,
even when life spins,
too fast to feel.
Through every high and low,
His presence steadies me,
quiet,
kind,
constant.

What I have,
Who I am,
is marked by grace.

His mercy flows,
not loud,
but strong enough,
to carry me.

In Him,
I find rest.
In His goodness,
I stand.

THE LOVE OF GOD

In the quiet of the morning,
I sit with question,
I can't answer.
But *"O The Love of God"*,
it calms the restless places in me.

Your love is light,
in dark places.
An anchor,
when waves rise high.

Through joy and sorrow,
You remain, constant,
kind, near.

I don't always
understand the path,
but I trust the One,
who walks with me.

You are my comfort.
You are my strength.

Your mercy is enough.
Your grace, my guide.
And in Your love,
I rest.

HAPPINESS

Happiness dances through the day,
In fields of gold where sunbeams play.
A gentle breeze, heartfelt smile,
Makes life worthwhile mile and mile.

Through stormy nights and cloudy skies,
Happiness still brightly shines.
In love that's pure, in moments shared,
It shows in how much we have cared.

In kindness shown to strangers' eyes,
In dreams that reach the boundless skies.
Happiness a guiding light,
Illuminates the darkest night.

So let us cherish every day,
Find happiness in our own way.
In deeds of love both big and small,
For happiness resides in all.

LAUGHTER

They say laughter is the best medicine,
and I believe it.
It softens the hard edges of life,
lifting sorrow, even if just for a moment.

It's more than a sound,
it's lightness in the chest,
a breath released,
a weight lifted without notice.

Laughter is a kind of healing,
a quiet magic that lives in the small things.
It doesn't fix everything,
but it makes the road easier to walk.

I try to begin each day,
with a smile, a laugh,
a bit of brightness I can share.

Not everyone understands,
some pull back,
mistaking joy for foolishness.
But I carry on.
Their silence isn't my burden.
The day moves forward, and so do I.

Laughter is a treasure,
a piece of joy we offer freely.
Without it, even the warmest gathering
feels just a little cold.

Let laughter live loudly in your life.
A chuckle, a deep belly laugh,
even a silly grin,
they're all reminders that we are alive,
and that joy is still within reach.

Laughter is the sunshine
we carry with us.
Let it rise.
Let it stay.

BE THANKFUL

The morning light touches your face,
soft, steady, and unspoken.
It asks quietly:
What fills your heart today?

Is it the weight of what you own?
Or the stillness of simple moments,
the quiet, steady pulse of being alive?

What stirs your soul with real gratitude?
The race for more,
a future not yet yours?
Or the beauty already here,
sun on your skin,
a voice that says your name with love?

Do you give thanks
for what money cannot buy,
the breath you take,
the sky above,
the people who see you as you are?

Are you awake to the small wonders,
the laughter that finds you,
the strength that carries you through,
the chance to begin again,
with each new morning?

Be thankful for now.
For the life still moving through you.
For what has been,
and what could still be.

Let gratitude shape your days,
quietly, deeply,
like a river running,
beneath everything you do.

EPILOGUE

In the end, life is not measured by years alone, but by the love we gave, the courage we carried, and the memories we leave behind. My journey has been one of shadows and light, of deep valleys and wide horizons, yet each step has shaped the person I have become.

Retirement has brought with it both stillness and renewal, a reminder that even as one chapter closes, another quietly begins. I face the future with thankfulness - cherishing family, friendships, and the gift of time.

My Life Journey is not finished here; it continues in the hearts of those I love, in the laughter of generations, and in the quiet strength found each new day.